Fairytales — and — Fables

Contents

CLIVEDEN PRESS

Dick Whittington

In the days when King Edward III sat upon the throne of England, there lived in a small village, some miles distant from London, a poor youth named Dick Whittington.

Dick had lost his parents at an early age, and now the orphaned boy lived as best he could, begging a crust or a bowl of gruel from anyone who might have a little to spare. But times were hard for the poor folk of the village, and often Dick went hungry to his bed in a corner of the stable of the village inn.

But he was a bright lad and he tried to learn from the visitors to the inn all he could about the wide world outside. He particularly loved the tales of London, with the talk of fine lords and ladies, music and dancing and strolling players.

When, one day, a passing waggoner told Dick that the streets of London were paved with gold coins, Dick finally decided to go off to London to seek his fortune.

He set off with a light heart, for the landlord's wife had packed him a little bread and cheese and a bottle of goat's milk for the journey. But the road was long and hard, and soon Dick had no food left.

He walked the last few miles to London, hungry, tired and footsore, and it was only the thought of the golden pavements which carried his feet on their way.

But, alas for poor Dick, he found no gold at his journey's end. The streets of London were just as dirty as the cart tracks on the village farms, and search hard as he might he could not find even one small coin of the realm, much less a golden guinea!

The streets were thronged with people going about their daily business, gentlefolk in carriages or accompanied on foot by servants, tradesmen selling their wares and a number of dirty-faced urchins who sped through the crowds at a speed which Dick found quite bewildering.

The smell of food wafting from several stalls made Dick feel quite faint, and finally he stumbled and fell outside the doorway of a fine house.

The house belonged to a certain Mr. Fitzwarren, a rich merchant who lived there with his wife and his daughter, Alice, and a number of servants.

As it happened, just as Dick fell, the door opened and Mr. Fitzwarren stepped out. He looked in some surprise at the figure on his doorstep.

At first he took Dick for an idle rogue, but as the boy stammered out his plight, the kindly merchant was filled with pity.

He told a servant to take Dick into the kitchen, give him a good meal and then let Dick help the cook in the kitchen with the rough work.

Dick could scarcely believe in his good fortune.

"Oh, thank you, sir, you will never regret it!" he cried.

As the days passed Dick worked long hours in the kitchen, trying to please the sharp-tongued cook. But she had a very bad temper, and often she would hit Dick with a long ladle or a broom if something had displeased her, even if it was not Dick's fault.

One day she was scolding Dick when Mistress Alice, the merchant's daughter, walked into the kitchen. Alice was a pretty girl with a kind heart, and she had also noticed how hard Dick worked, always trying to stay willing and cheerful despite the cook's harsh treatment of him.

"If you do not treat Dick better than this, you had better look for another situation, Cook!" said Alice, firmly.

And from that day on, things began to get better for Dick in the kitchen.

But although the cook was now much kinder to Dick, he still had another problem. The garret room in which he slept was overrun with rats and mice which constantly disturbed his sleep, and made him feel very tired when he had to get up in the morning.

One day, just after Mr. Fitzwarren had given Dick a penny for giving his shoes an extra shine, Dick told Kate the kitchen maid, about the mice in the garret.

"Buy a cat with your penny!" cried Kate at once. "Puss will soon get rid of your mice and rats."

"I will!" answered Dick.

Dick found a magnificent black cat to share his garret, and soon there was not one mouse to be seen!

Now Dick felt very contented with his life. He had a good job, plenty of food and a cat of his own for company.

One morning Mr. Fitzwarren called all his servants in to see him.

"My ship is ready to sail with its cargo to foreign parts," said the merchant. "If any of you have any goods which you would like to send on the voyage, my captain will take them on board and sell them for you at the best price he can obtain."

All the servants were pleased to hear this. They all had something to give to the captain, except poor Dick who had neither money nor goods.

Mistress Alice noticed how this distressed Dick, and suddenly she had an idea.

"Send your cat, Dick!" cried Alice. "Perhaps someone will buy him, for he is a magnificent creature."

So, sadly, Dick said goodbye to his cat, amid laughter from all the company. Kindhearted Alice gave Dick a penny to buy another cat to keep the garret free from mice and rats.

But Dick missed Puss very much, and because the cook could see how fond Mistress Alice was of Dick, the cook treated him very cruelly and made fun of him for sending his cat away to sea.

Each day Dick grew more and more unhappy, until at last he decided to leave London and return home to his village.

"All my fine plans have come to nothing," he murmured to himself. "And how I shall miss dear Mistress Alice!"

While it was still dark on the morning of All Hallows' Day, Dick packed his few belongings up in a large kerchief, knotted this to a stick, and crept out of the house.

He had not gone very far when he sat down on a milestone to decide which of the four crossroads he should take.

Suddenly Dick heard the bells of Bow Church begin to ring, and they seemed to be sending him a message:

"Turn again, Whittington,
Thrice Lord Mayor of London!"

"Lord Mayor of London!" cried Dick. "If one day I will ride in a fine coach as Lord Mayor of London then I will go back! I will take no notice of the cook's sharp tongue. One day she will respect me!"

And Dick hurried back to the merchant's house before anyone else was up and had realised that he had gone out.

Meanwhile, the merchant's ship had been driven off-course in a very bad storm. When the storm abated the captain found himself on a part of the Barbary coast where he had never been before.

The people there were black-skinned Moors, and when the captain and his crew landed they welcomed the sailors warmly, and asked to see what goods they had brought.

When they saw the bales of silks and satin cloth the natives told the captain to go and call at the royal palace to show their goods to the King and Queen.

The King and Queen were delighted to see the captain and his crew and they gave a banquet in their honour. Everyone sat on richly-embroidered cushions at a low table which was covered with exotic meats and fruits.

Everyone was just starting to eat when suddenly in rushed a plague of rats and mice and began to devour the food with their sharp teeth.

The captain watched in horror, and the King and Queen were very ashamed at what had happened before their guests.

"I would give anything to get rid of these vermin!" cried the King. "They eat our food, disturb our sleep and frighten our children!"

"Your Majesty, I have a creature aboard my ship who will get rid of all your mice and rats!" cried the captain, and he sent a sailor to bring Dick's cat back to the royal court.

"If what you say is true, you shall have as much gold and jewels as your ship will carry if I can keep this creature!" shouted the King.

A short time later Puss arrived. How his eyes gleamed when he saw all those rats and mice! He jumped out onto the table and soon the King's troubles were over!

"We must have this creature," cried the Queen, clapping her hands in delight. "He is called a cat, you say? And his name is Puss? Here . . . Puss!"

And sly old Puss climbed onto the Queen's lap, purring gently, while the King's servants filled many large sacks with gold and jewels for the captain and his men to take back to their ship.

"Well, Puss has certainly found a grand home for himself," laughed the captain, as he set sail for home.

"Aye, Cap'n, and he has earned young Whittington a small fortune," cried the ship's mate. "Imagine, all this wealth for a cat which cost just one penny."

"Yes, but it was worth much more to the King. Now he can eat and sleep in peace," replied the captain. "Puss will keep those rats in order!"

The merchant ship had a fair wind all the way home, and soon it docked once again in London.

The captain hurried to Mr. Fitzwarren's counting house to tell him the good news. First he told the merchant how he had sold all Mr. Fitzwarren's goods at a very fair price. Then he told him all about the cat which he had exchanged for gold and jewels.

Mr. Fitzwarren was very pleased to hear of Dick's good fortune. "He shall receive every penny," he vowed. "I will return home and tell him of the news myself. I am truly happy for the boy, for he is good and honest and I have always like him."

Dick could scarcely contain his joy when he saw all the gold and jewels. At once he gave some to the captain and crew, and he even gave a gold ring to the ill-natured old cook.

Mr. Fitzwarren offered to help Dick look after his money and, knowing him to be a just and wise man, Dick willingly agreed to this.

Mr. Fitzwarren also took Dick to his tailor's, where Dick bought clothes to befit his new life, and he stayed at the merchant's house as an honoured guest for several months.

Now that he had position and wealth Dick felt that he could ask Alice to marry him, for he loved her dearly. Alice accepted happily and, with her father's full approval, they were married.

A great feast followed the wedding, which was attended by the Lord Mayor, the court of aldermen, the sheriffs and many rich merchants of the city of London.

Yes, that, too, came true. The young country lad did become Lord Mayor of London . . . three times, just as the bells had foretold.

And today, if you ever visit Westminster Abbey, you will see a stained glass window of Dick Whittington and his cat . . . proof that *sometimes* fairy tales *do* come true!

The FROG PRINCE

Once, long ago, in the days of magic and enchantment, there lived a king who had a lovely daughter. She lived with her father in a magnificent castle near a dense forest.

In the middle of the forest stood an old lime tree, beneath whose branches splashed a silver fountain which ran into a deep pool.

On a warm day the princess, whose name was Melanie, would take her favourite toy, a golden ball, and go off to play in the forest under the lime tree, where it was cool and shady.

The princess would throw her golden ball up into the air and catch it again, or sometimes she would toss it against the tree and catch it again as it bounced back.

One warm summer's day Princess Melanie was playing her favourite game with her golden ball, when suddenly, instead of catching it, the ball slipped from the princess's fingers and disappeared into the deep waters of the pool.

Princess Melanie gazed in dismay into the water and then she began to cry.

"What shall I do?" she sobbed aloud.

Suddenly a frog popped out of the water and, to the princess's surprise and amazement, the frog spoke to her.

"Princess, why are you weeping?" asked the frog.

"Alas, my golden ball has fallen into the pool," replied Princess Melanie sadly. "I would give all my jewels to get it back . . . even my golden crown."

"I will dive into the pool and bring back your golden ball," cried the frog at once. "But I want neither your jewels nor your crown as my reward. All I ask is that you will love me and let me be your dear companion, eating from your golden plate and sleeping upon your bed. If you agree to this, you shall have your ball."

"No slimy green frog shall ever eat from my plate!" thought the princess to herself. "A frog eat with a princess indeed! Let him stay in the pool where he belongs and feed upon worms!"

But aloud she cried, "Of course I agree, dear frog. I promise it shall be as you wish . . . just bring me back my ball."

So the frog dived into the pool and brought back the golden ball.

But as he dropped it at her feet the princess seized the golden ball and ran off quickly towards the royal castle.

"Stop, stop! Princess, wait for me!" called the frog. "Remember your promise!"

But Princess Melanie pretended not to hear as she ran swiftly through the trees, leaving the frog far behind her.

"That horrid frog will never dare to follow me here," murmured the princess to herself as she reached the castle safely, running past the royal guards and shutting the door firmly behind her.

But that night, as the princess sat at dinner eating from her own golden plate, she heard a strange noise, as if something was hopping up the marble staircase outside the room.

There was a knock at the door and a voice cried, "Daughter of the king, open the door!"

Feeling very frightened the princess arose and opened the door . . . and there stood the small green frog.

The princess slammed the door shut and went back to her place at the table.

But her father, the king, could see that something was amiss, and he asked her what was wrong.

Almost in tears the princess told the king about losing her golden ball and of her promise to the frog if he returned it.

As she finished speaking, the frog knocked again, calling out:

"Open the door, Princess dear,
I promise you, you have nought to fear.
But remember the promise you made to me,
When you lost your ball 'neath the old lime tree."

"A promise is a promise," said the king, gravely. "Let him in."

And so the princess had to open the door for the frog to come in, and she had to lift him onto the table so that they could eat together from her golden plate.

The frog ate heartily. But Princess Melanie could not touch a morsel, for she felt any food might choke her because she was so upset about sharing her meal with a frog!

When the meal was over the frog said that he was tired and, despite all her pleas, the king commanded his daughter to carry the frog upstairs to bed.

"You are a princess and a royal promise must be kept," said the king, sternly.

At first the princess hid the frog in a clothes closet, but he cried so loudly that she was forced to let him out in case her father heard his cries and was angry at what she had done. The princess had to let the frog sleep on her pillow all night.

But when dawn broke the frog had gone.

"I hope that's the last we shall see of him," murmured the princess as she got out of bed.

But for the next two nights the frog returned, to eat from her golden plate and to sleep on the princess's pillow until morning light.

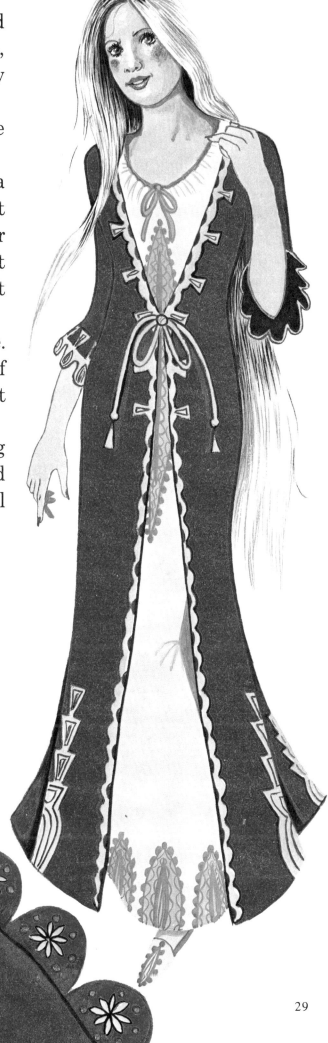

But on the morning following the third night, the princess awoke to find a handsome prince standing by her bed.

"Are you the frog?" faltered Princess Melanie in amazement.

"I was a frog," replied the prince. "A cruel spell was put upon me by a wicked witch who forced me to remain a frog until a real princess let me eat from her plate and sleep on her bed for three nights. But now I am free, and all I wish is for you to consent to be my bride before I return to my own kingdom."

It did not take Princess Melanie very long to decide to marry the prince, because he was very handsome and she soon discovered that he also had a very kind heart.

They were married with great pomp and rejoicing before driving away to the prince's kingdom in a splendid carriage drawn by eight white horses, each horse bedecked in a solid gold bridle and wearing a plume of ostrich feathers upon its head.

The Hare
and the Tortoise

The Hare was a vain, boastful creature. He loved the sound of his own voice so he was always talking. Yak, yak, yak, all day long!

He thought there was no one to touch him. No one could run as he did, no one could jump as he did, and how he showed off! Without warning, he would run up a tree or stand on his head, expecting all the other animals to applaud his cleverness. He could talk of nothing but himself and what he could do. He went on and on and on. . .

At last, the other animals, who at first had thought him rather

clever, began to grow tired of his boasting and showing off. Day after day, day after day, it was the same. He really was a most troublesome creature.

One day, when Hare had gone to visit his Aunt (and he would tell the others *all* about it when he returned) the birds and animals gathered together to talk about the silly fellow and to stop him becoming a bore.

"We must teach him a lesson," said Rabbit.

"A good idea," agreed the others, "but what can we do?"

They all thought and thought but no one could think of a single idea.

The squirrel, who had been dozing in his tree, suddenly sat up and shouted, "I've got it! I know what to do!"

"Tell us," begged the others, "what can we do?"

"Let's go and see Tortoise," said Squirrel. "After all, he's slow, but he's very old and wise."

The Tortoise had a stall in the Market Place and sold vegeta-

bles very cheaply. He had been doing this as long as he could remember, and that was a very, very long time, for he was over a hundred years old. When he reached his one hundredth birthday, he had stopped counting, and so had all the others, so no one knew his real age. Everyone went to him for advice — except Hare of course.

The sun was warm and business was slow so Tortoise was dozing in the shade when he was surprised to see all the animals approaching his stall. At first, he thought they had come to buy until Rabbit explained they had come for his help. Tortoise was flattered.

"It's about Hare," said Squirrel.

"Naturally, who else?" replied Tortoise.

"We have just about had enough of the tiresome fellow," they all chorused, "but what can we do?"

"Ah, yes," said Tortoise gravely, "I have been expecting you."

"What do you suggest?" asked Rabbit.

"I must think," said Tortoise. He closed his eyes and held up a foot for silence. It looked as if he was sleeping, but everyone knew he did his best thinking with his eyes shut. It was the best way to concentrate!

At long last, he blinked and opened his eyes.

"I think I have an excellent plan," he said.

They all gathered eagerly round and listened as he explained. When he had finished no one said a word.

"I only hope it works," said Squirrel doubtfully.

"It will," said Tortoise. "I know our friend, Hare."

When Hare returned he was surprised to see Tortoise holding forth, and wondered what all the fuss was about. He soon knew, for later Tortoise called to see him.

"I want to challenge you to a race," said Tortoise quietly.

"A-- what?" cried the startled Hare. "A race!" He began to laugh, for Tortoise was the slowest fellow on legs.

"I have told everyone that I am racing you. We shall start from

Hog's Meadow and race to Peascod Pasture tomorrow morning at nine o'clock," said the Tortoise. "All right?"

"Are you sure you feel well, old man?" asked Hare.

"I am very well, thank you," smiled Tortoise. "Till tomorrow, my friend."

Next morning everyone, but everyone, was waiting in Hog's Meadow long before nine o'clock to watch the race.

"It is quite ridiculous," said Hare, feeling a bit silly, "an awful waste of my time," he went on, limbering up.

"Oh, I don't think so," said Tortoise who had arrived.

"I only hope Tortoise doesn't fall asleep," said Rabbit rather anxiously, "you know how he drops off when the sun is warm, and it looks like being a hot day." He frowned at the blue sky.

Secretly, the animals were worried at the Tortoise's plan, but he was very calm.

Rabbit acted as starter. "Ready, steady, GO!" he shouted and, to a great cheer from all the animals, the race started. Hare lolloped along with a very superior grin all over his face and was soon out of sight.

Tortoise plodded along slowly. His friends cheered him on, "Go on, Tortoise! Do hurry up!"

Rabbit and Squirrel, too impatient to wait, jumped on bicycles and pedalled after Hare.

Tortoise padded on steadily. If his plan worked, he had plenty of time.

Hare was soon hot and thirsty. When he came to a cool stream, he stopped and had a long, refreshing drink. Just then, Squirrel and Rabbit arrived. "You go on, Squirrel," said Rabbit, "my tyres are flat and I must pump them up. Why, hello, Hare," he said, "having a drink?"

Hare licked his lips. "That's better," he said. "I think I'll take a swim now, I have plenty of time."

Rabbit pumped up his tyres and Hare watched him. "Are you taking a long rest?" he asked.

"I am in no hurry," boasted Hare, "I am in such good form, it's all the carrots and lettuce I eat."

Just then, plodding steadily along, Tortoise appeared in the path. "Well, I never, old slow-coach," laughed Hare and raced off chuckling to himself.

He was soon out of sight. On and on he ran until he felt hungry. He came to a sweet scented patch of clover too tasty to miss, and, settling himself comfortably against a tree, ate a huge lunch.

He had nothing to worry about, Tortoise could not possibly win the race and was probably fast asleep in the sun by now, anyway.

It was a beautiful day. The sun shone and Hare closed his eyes. He was fast asleep when Tortoise slowly passed by at his steady pace.

Hare slept for a long time. His huge lunch and swim had tired him and the hot sun made him sleepy. Waking with a start, he remembered the race. The sun was still high in the sky and he would have loved to rest a little longer. He looked up and down but there was no sign of the Tortoise, so with a sigh he set off again.

Round the next bend he stopped short in amazement. By the side of the path was a most wonderful cake. A huge, iced cake, all by itself. And how Hare loved cake! No one was in sight, and it would melt in the sun. Quickly, he dug his teeth into a slice, then another and another, until only crumbs were left for the birds.

With a great spurt, Hare raced over the last fields to the finishing line. He was astounded to see Tortoise being cheered past the post! Everyone was clapping and waving excitedly. Tortoise had won!

Hare rushed up. "What happened?" he cried, "I don't understand it. Everyone knows I can run faster than Tortoise, any day!"

"You may be able to run faster," Tortoise agreed, "but you can't think faster." And he began to laugh. Soon all the animals, even Hare, who was quite good-natured really, deep down, laughed with him. "It was a good cake," he spluttered and went home to think.

Hare is a changed person now and everyone likes him. As for Tortoise, he still has his stall and smiles to himself when he thinks of how he bested Hare.

The REAL PRINCESS

Once upon a time there was a Prince who wished to marry a Princess. But she had to be a *real* Princess, so he travelled around the whole world trying to find one. Now there were plenty of Princesses, but he could not quite satisfy himself that any of them was a real Princess, for there was something about each of them that did not seem quite right.

Finally the Prince returned home without a bride. But he was sad, for he very much wanted to marry a real Princess.

One night, about a week after he returned, there was a terrible storm. Thunder rolled and lightning darted across the dark sky, and then the rain poured down in torrents.

When the storm was at its height there came a loud knocking at the gate of the castle. Protected by a courtier who carried a very large umbrella, the old King went out to see who was at the gate.

A young and very beautiful girl stood outside. But what a state she was in! Water ran down her face like giant teardrops and her fair hair clung to her head like a silken cap. The rain dripped in at the heels of her shoes and dribbled out at the toes, and her clothes hung, sodden and shapeless, around her. But even in this wet state she was beautiful and, to the Prince's amazement and joy, she claimed that she was a *real* Princess.

But the old Queen was cautious in her judgements. "We'll soon find out," she thought.

She said nothing but went up to the bedroom where the girl would be sleeping. Taking all the clothes off the bed she put a small pea on the mattress. Then on top of this mattress she heaped twenty more mattresses and then twenty eiderdown quilts. Then she remade the bed with its embroidered sheets and soft pink blankets.

When all was ready she called the Princess. "Sleep well, my dear," she said as she left her to settle down for the night.

It was the Prince who met the girl as she came down the stairs the following morning, and he asked her how she had rested.

At first she was reluctant to complain about the hospitality of her hosts.

But finally, when pressed, she admitted: "I have scarcely closed my eyes the whole night. I don't know what can have been in my bed, but I lay upon something hard, so that my whole body is black and blue. It was really dreadful."

It was evident then that the beautiful girl *was* a real Princess, since nobody but a Princess could have such a fine sense of feeling as to be bruised by one pea through twenty mattresses and twenty eiderdown quilts.

So the Prince married her. And the pea . . . well, it was placed in the royal museum, where it may still be seen if nobody has taken it away.

Tom Thumb

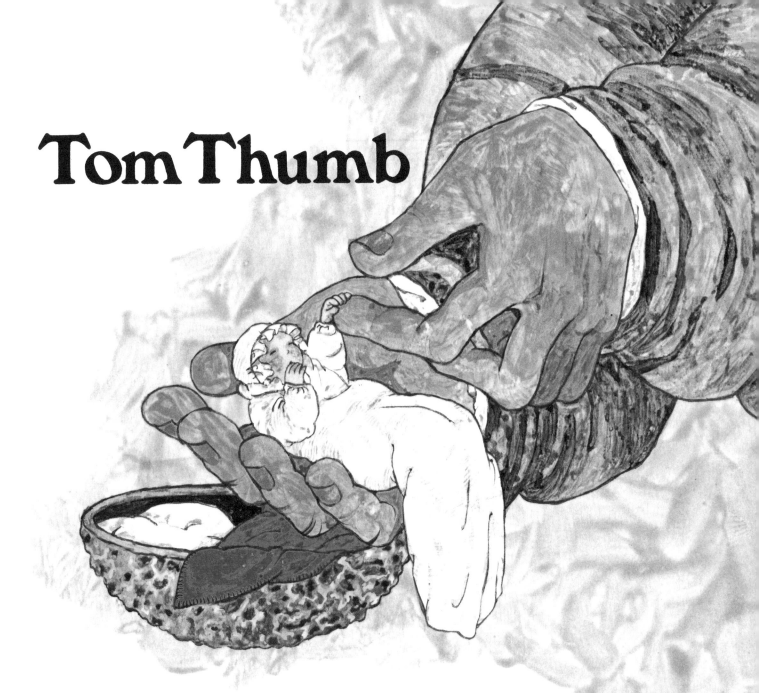

There was once a poor woodcutter who lived with his wife in a tiny cottage at the edge of a wood. One night as he sat by the fire, with his wife sitting by his side spinning, the man said, "How lonely it is, sitting here by ourselves, without any children to play about and amuse us. Other people seem so happy and merry with their children."

"What you say is true, husband," replied his wife, sighing as she turned her spinning wheel. "I should be happy with only one child. Even if it were no bigger than my thumb, I should love it dearly!"

Now shortly after this the good woman's wish was fulfilled, and she had a little boy who, although healthy and strong, was no bigger than her thumb.

"Well, we have got the son that we wished for," said the woodcutter's wife, "and small though he is, we shall love him dearly."

Because of his size, the couple named their son Tom Thumb.

Although they gave their son plenty of good food, Tom remained the same size as when he was born. But his eyes were sharp and sparkling and he soon showed that he was a clever little fellow despite his small size.

One day as the woodcutter was getting ready to go into the wood to cut some logs, he said, "If I had someone to come after me with the cart, I need not wait for it to be harnessed, and I could get on with my work better."

"Father, let me take care of the cart!" cried Tom. "I promise you I shall be in the wood by the time you need it!"

"But how can that be, Tom?" said his father. "You cannot reach the donkey's bridle."

"If my mother will harness the donkey, I will climb into the animal's ear, and tell him which way to go, as we travel along."

"Well, we can but try," agreed his father.

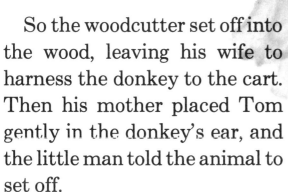

So the woodcutter set off into the wood, leaving his wife to harness the donkey to the cart. Then his mother placed Tom gently in the donkey's ear, and the little man told the animal to set off.

The donkey obeyed Tom and away they rode, with Tom issuing various orders as they travelled along.

The cart passed by two strangers who were very surprised to see a cart driven by a carter who could be heard but not seen.

"This is very strange," one said to the other. "Let's follow this cart and see where it goes."

So the strangers travelled behind the cart until it came to the place in the wood where Tom's father was working.

When Tom saw his father, standing beside a pile of logs, he called out: "Here I am, Father, with the cart, all safe and sound! Please help me down now!"

So his father held the donkey steady with one hand while he took Tom out of the animal's ear. The woodcutter set Tom down on a tiny log where he chatted away to his father as merrily as you please.

As the two strangers looked at the tiny boy they had an idea, and they started whispering to each other.

"This boy could make our fortune if we showed him off from town to town," one said.

"Aye, let's offer to buy him!" replied his companion.

And they went over to ask Tom's father how much he would take in return for his son.

"What, sell my own flesh and blood? Never!" cried Tom's father, and he glared angrily at the two strangers.

But as they turned to talk together yet again, Tom crept up his father's coat to his shoulder and whispered in his ear.

"Take the money, Father," he said softly, "and let them have me. Don't worry, I shall soon be back with you."

So the woodcutter agreed to give Tom to the strangers for one large piece of gold.

One of the men placed Tom on the wide brim of his hat, from where Tom had a good view of the road. Then off they set.

As dusk fell, the strangers stopped for a while at the side of the road. The man took off his hat and set Tom down on a clod of earth in a ploughed field near an opening in the hedge.

Quick as a trice Tom ran about among the furrows until at last he found an old mousehole. He slipped quickly into it.

"Come out of there, you young rascal!" cried the men, poking into the hole with sticks. "We have paid good money for you!"

But clever young Tom just crawled further and further into the hole and, as it grew dark, the strangers were forced to give up and continue on their way, muttering angrily about being cheated out of their bargain.

When he was quite sure that the strangers had gone, Tom crept out of his hole and began to search for a more comfortable bed in which to spend the night.

Luckily, Tom found an empty snail shell, which he lined with soft moss. There he slept sweetly until daybreak.

"Now at last, I am free to return home," said Tom to himself as he drank the dew which had settled upon a clover leaf.

But, alas for Tom's hopes! It was to be many a long day before he saw his parents again for, as he walked along the highway, whistling merrily, a raven swooped down and picked up poor Tom and flew away with him over the sea, where the bird dropped the little man.

A large fish caught Tom in his mouth and the little mannikin found himself falling down and down into the fish's stomach.

"Well, this is a pretty pickle! What is to become of me now?" murmured Tom, as he gazed around him in the darkness.

But once again good fortune smiled upon Tom, for shortly afterwards the fish was caught and taken to the royal kitchens as a gift for the king.

When the cook opened up the fish to cook it, out popped Tom, delighted to see daylight once more.

The cook was speechless with amazement at the first sight of Tom. But when she had recovered her senses, she washed the little man in a teacup of soapy water, dried him out, and then took him along to see the king.

The king and queen were delighted to see such a handsome little fellow and they ordered the royal tailor to make a fine suit of clothes for Tom. The royal hatter made Tom an elegant cap with a feather, and the royal shoemaker produced a pair of shoes for him made from the finest leather.

Tom soon became a firm favourite with everyone at court. He went hunting with the king and he sang sweetly for the queen when her musicians played for her in the royal gardens.

He also played games with the royal pages. But one day when he was playing cherry stones with Crispin, the royal page noticed that although Tom was losing, he still had lots of stones.

Then Crispin saw that Tom was slipping into the page's bag and stealing stones when Crispin wasn't looking.

So Crispin decided to teach Tom a lesson!

He waited until Tom was once more in the cherry stone bag, and then he drew the bag strings together tightly, and gave the stones a big shake.

Poor Tom's legs and shoulders were very badly bruised, and he promised never to cheat at games again!

One day the king asked Tom about his parents. On hearing that the woodcutter and his wife were poor and that Tom longed to see his dear mother and father once again to tell them that he was still alive and living at the royal court, the king suggested that Tom went home for a visit and took his parents some money.

The king took Tom along to the royal treasury and told Tom that he could take home as much money as he could carry.

"Oh, thank you, sire!" cried Tom. He searched through the pockets of his suit until he found his purse which was made of a water-bubble. Then he took a large sixpenny piece and pushed it into his purse.

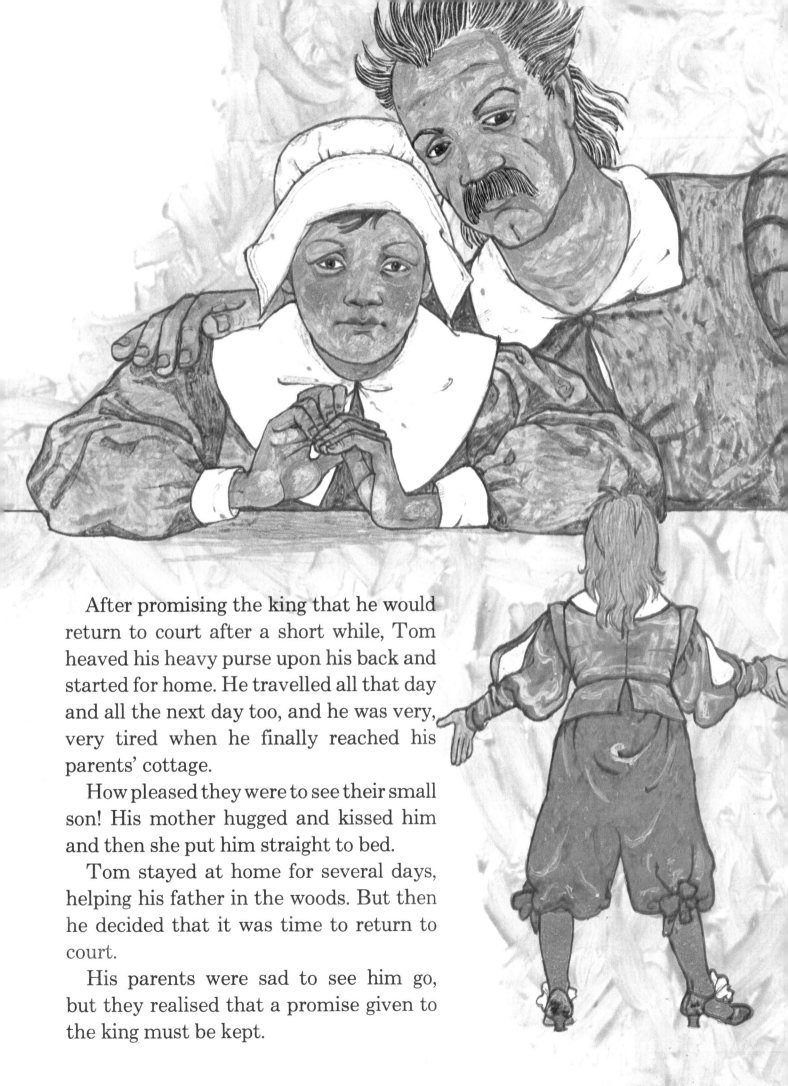

After promising the king that he would return to court after a short while, Tom heaved his heavy purse upon his back and started for home. He travelled all that day and all the next day too, and he was very, very tired when he finally reached his parents' cottage.

How pleased they were to see their small son! His mother hugged and kissed him and then she put him straight to bed.

Tom stayed at home for several days, helping his father in the woods. But then he decided that it was time to return to court.

His parents were sad to see him go, but they realised that a promise given to the king must be kept.

So his mother made him a tiny umbrella from gossamer thread and, with Tom holding tightly to the handle, she blew it gently towards the royal palace.

Just as Tom was floating down into the royal courtyard the cook was crossing over the yard on her way to the royal apartments to give the king a bowl of porridge for his breakfast.

Down floated Tom Thumb, right into the centre of the bowl of porridge and splattered the cook from head to toe with the sticky stuff.

"Oh, you naughty, naughty Tom Thumb!" she shouted, and rushed off to complain to the king about poor Tom.

The king was very busy with affairs of state that day and so the cook put poor Tom into a wire mousetrap and kept him there.

It was a whole week before the king remembered about poor Tom Thumb, and when he heard about the mousetrap, the king felt very sorry for Tom and he granted him a royal pardon.

In order to please both Tom and the cook, both of whose clothes had been ruined by the porridge, the king ordered new clothes for both of them.

When the cook saw how fine *she* looked in her new dress, she forgave Tom for falling into the porridge, and she asked *him* to forgive her for putting him in the mousetrap!

Tom looked so fine in his new clothes that the king said that, despite his small size, Tom was worthy to become one of his knights.

The king knighted Tom with a silver darning needle which afterwards Sir Thomas always used as his trusty sword. The court jester even made a song up about Tom and sang it around the court:

"Of silk and satin are Tom's clothes made,
His boots are of fine leather hide;
His sword, a handsome needle blade,
While a snow-white mouse he doth ride."

One day the fairy queen came to the king's court, and she asked Tom to return to Fairy-land with her for a visit, for Queen Mab had watched over Tom from the day he was born.

Sir Thomas was delighted to visit the land of the fairies, especially as most of them were only as tall as himself.

He stayed there for a long time and when he returned to court he brought back with him many fairy gifts.

The king was delighted and pleased to see his dear friend, Sir Thomas, back once again at the royal court. He ordered a tiny golden chair to be made so that Tom could sit and eat at the royal table. The king also gave Tom a tiny coach drawn by six small mice, so that he could travel in style whenever he visited his parents.

And so Tom Thumb, a noble knight even though he was no bigger than his mother's thumb, lived happily for many years, and was known throughout the land for his bravery and his wit.

Prince Ahmed and the Princess

Long, long ago in old Persia there lived a rich Sultan named Omar and his lovely daughter, the Princess Nurina, who was the apple of his eye.

She was so beautiful that many Princes from the neighbouring kingdoms sought her hand in marriage, but she refused them all. They spent their time in idleness, eating and drinking and courting her favours, but she found them very dull and refused to marry any of those who tried to win her. She longed for a man with courage and skill, not a Court flatterer who was a coward at heart. Her father, the Sultan, understood and shared her feelings.

One day, Ahmed, a Prince from a far off land, lost his way while out hunting and came to the Sultan's Palace for rest and refreshment.

He soon learned of Princess Nurina and her loveliness which he wanted to see for himself.

"May I see your daughter?" he asked the Sultan the next day. "No one may see my daughter unless he can prove himself a man of strength and determination and one who is worthy of her," the Sultan replied.

"Won't you even let me just look at her?" begged the Prince.

The Sultan remained firm and Prince Ahmed gathered his retinue together and rode sorrowfully on his way.

But he was now determined to find a way of proving his worthiness to win the hand of the Princess, athough he knew many had tried and failed.

As Prince Ahmed rode on he remembered, how, many years ago at his father's Court, he had talked with an aged soothsayer who had told him of strange things.

"In the years to come you will seek a beautiful bride, but to win her you must first find three things. You will need a magic telescope which can see everything, even through walls, a magic carpet to fly you wherever you wish and a magic bow and arrow which will never fail you."

"But where will I find such things?" asked the Prince.

"Seek for the telescope in a remote city, in the house of a merchant, hidden in an old trunk. Then journey on to a lonely village where you will discover a small carpet, green in colour with a red and yellow pattern. When you have these things, you will see the bow and arrow."

Then Ahmed knew what the must do. He set out.

After journeying for many miles with much fruitless search-

ing, Prince Ahmed reached an old, remote city whose very walls seemd to hold the secrets of the past. This must be the place, he thought, and looked for the house of the merchant.

The merchant's son told him his father had had an old telescope stored away somewhere, given him by a magician who said a young man would come for it one day. He promised to find it for the Prince. "Come back in three days," he said, "and I will have it ready for you."

In three days Ahmed returned and was shown a very old telescope, painted a dull red. This must be the one, he thought excitedly, and paid the merchant two gold pieces.

The merchant also had a bow for sale but somehow the Prince knew it was not the magic one.

"Next find the carpet," thought Ahmed and, looking through the telescope, he saw a tiny village in the far distance. Night was falling, but he knew his search for the carpet had ended.

A carpet dealer said he thought he had the very one he wanted — small, green, with an unusual red and yellow pattern on it, which would carry him where he pleased. The deal completed, the Prince and his servant quickly climbed on to the carpet and commanded it to fly. In a moment, they were airborne, riding high above the desert.

Looking through the telescope, Ahmed saw an archer with a large bow slung across his shoulders. Instinctively he knew this was the magic one and quickly descended to buy it.

Airborne once more, Ahmed flew towards the city and as he approached the Sultan's Palace, he saw one of the Viziers pacing up and down looking very worried.

"Descend," he ordered the carpet, and approached the Vizier.

"Why are you so unhappy?" he asked.

"It is the Princess Nurina," the Vizier replied, "she is ill, pining away, but no one can help her."

"What is wrong?" asked Ahmed in concern.

"An Evil Spirit has cast a spell on her which cannot be broken," said the Vizier, "everyone has tried."

"Let me try," begged Ahmed, "I think I know the secret of how to do it."

"Well, it can do no harm," said the Vizier, "come with me."

"I have three magic things," Ahmed told him, "a telescope with which I can see anything, even through a wall, a magic carpet which brought me here and a bow and arrow which never misses its target."

Ahmed looked through his telescope and immediately saw the Evil Spirit standing on a high turret overlooking the Palace, his gaze fixed on the Princess. The Spirit, who was very cunning, instinctively knew he was being spied on and looked around to see who was looking at him.

At that moment, the Princess, released from his evil gaze, began to stir from her long sleep and open her eyes. The Sultan called everyone to her bedside.

"Nurina wakes! She is well!" He clapped his hands in delight. "Thanks be to Allah."

Seeing Prince Ahmed, the Evil Spirit flew into a great rage. With a terrifying look he started to descend from the turret towards Prince Ahmed.

Hurriedly, the Prince dropped the telescope and picked up the bow and arrow. Fixing the arrow into his bow he shot it high into the air. The arrow first flew on a straight course but then, suddenly, it turned in the direction of the Evil Spirit.

Just then, the Sultan and Nurina came out into the courtyard, looking for the stranger their Vizier had told them about. It was a strange sight that met their eyes.

"Ah!" screamed the Evil Spirit as the arrow struck him between

the eyes, transfixing him to a stone parapet. With an ear-splitting shriek, he was consumed in a ball of fire and was never seen again.

The Sultan and his daughter had watched in amazement as the arrow changed its course to kill the Evil Spirit.

"It must be magic!" they cried. "Who can the archer be?"

Just then, Prince Ahmed entered the Palace, bow in hand, and asked to see the Sultan. The courtiers gathered round him offering their congratulations to this wonderful archer who had rid them of the Evil Spirit.

The Sultan stepped forward. He recognised the Prince as the man who had wished to see the Princess on his earlier visit.

"A welcome return!" cried Omar, "and my thanks for saving my daughter. You have earned the privilege of meeting her."

At first glance, Princess Nurina and Prince Ahmed knew their dreams were fulfilled. Turning to her father, she said, "I would like to marry this Prince who has proved himself so brave and resourceful."

The Sultan was delighted and straightway a grand wedding was planned.

People from far and wide came to join in the wedding celebrations and everyone was happy that their Princess was marrying so fine a Prince.

In all the excitement, the magic telescope, the carpet and the bow and arrow were forgotten and no one knew what happened to them. Nor did anyone really care now that all was well in the land!

The Lion and the Mouse

THE little grey mouse liked living in the jungle. There was so much to see: giant giraffes who were so far above him that conversation was a hopeless shouting game, friendly elephants whose feet he had to dodge carefully, and tiny ants who often disturbed his sleep as they swarmed over him on their busy march. It was safe, too, in the jungle. There were so many animals around that a careful little mouse could live quite a long and happy life.

But, one day, the little mouse, less careful than usual, made a fatal mistake. He ran over the paws of a sleeping lion.

Now the lion was very annoyed at being disturbed, especially by so insignificant a creature as a mouse. He gave a great roar and brought one of his mighty paws down on the offending mouse, flattening him to the ground.

The tiny mouse was very frightened. "Excuse me," he panted. "It was an accident, really it was."

The lion was tawny, and yawny, and terribly big. "A likely story!" he growled. "You woke me from a good sound sleep. And now I'm going to eat you up!"

"Please don't," begged the mouse. "I'm really much too young to die, and I do enjoy living. If you let me go, maybe someday *I* will be able to help *you!*"

"Help *me!*" the lion sneered. "Now how could a bit of grey fluff like you, help a powerful and fearsome creature like me? Answer me that!"

"I could swat the flies and keep them from pestering you," said the mouse.

"Who cares about flies?" snorted the lion.

"I could ride on your back through the jungle and tell you stories," said the mouse.

"And ruffle my beautiful mane?" roared the lion. "No, thank you."

"There must be something I could do," pleaded the mouse, "I'm very willing."

The lion laughed. He was normally quite a good-natured lion. "You may be small, but you have some courage. Run along then, before I change my mind."

As the lion lifted its paw the little mouse was off. "Remember," he called back, "if you ever need my help, just roar."

Weeks passed and the mouse was enjoying

life all the more for having nearly lost it. He played with the monkeys, dodged the elephants and went for a shower in the river on a hippo's back. But, in all his travels, he never met the lion.

Then, one afternoon, as all the animals were having their nap, a thunderous roar echoed through the jungle. The monkeys chattered excitedly, the birds left their nests and soared up into the safety of the sky. Only the mouse wasn't nervous.

"I'd know that roar anywhere," said the mouse. "It's my friend, the lion."

Then came another roar, even louder than before. It was not a happy sound either. There was no doubt about it, the lion was in trouble.

"Don't worry," squeaked the mouse, "I'm coming."

The little grey mouse followed the sound of the lion's roaring and eventually he found his friend, all tied up with ropes and looking very unhappy.

"Some hunters caught me in a trap," he explained, "and then tied me up. Soon they'll be back with a lorry to take me to the circus. Imagine ending up as a circus lion!" Tears ran down his shaggy face.

"That will never happen while I'm around," promised the mouse. "Now stay still and I'll soon have you free."

The mouse began to gnaw at the ropes with his sharp little teeth, breaking them strand by strand. It was hard work because the ropes were thick and tough. But, although he was thirsty and his front teeth ached with the effort, the little grey mouse did not give up.

At last, the final strand snapped and the lion was free again. He stretched and he stretched and he stretched.

"You may be small, little mouse," purred the happy lion, "but you have the heart of a lion. From now on the two of us will be the best of friends."

And they were.

A friend in need is a friend indeed, no matter how small he may be.

In the ancient kingdom of Greece there once lived a king called Midas. His kingdom was a rich and powerful one, and on the whole Midas was a good king, kind to his people and merciful in his judgements.

But Midas had one great fault: more than anything else in the world he loved gold. He collected and hoarded gold – as a woman gathers loving words, getting great happiness from just remembering them. He did not want to spend the gold, nor yet to give it away. He loved it not for the good he could do with it. No, Midas loved gold for the sake of the precious metal itself, cherishing it like a miser.

Every day he would spend hours in his treasure room, gazing at the gold and

The king who loved GOLD

letting it slip through his fingers in an ecstasy of joy. The thought of all his gold occupied most of his waking hours and some of his dreamtime too.

Some nights he would have happy dreams about all the golden beauty which he possessed; other nights he would wake up from a nightmare and hurry down to the treasure room in his nightgown, shaking from their sleep the six guards who looked after the treasure day and night.

Only when he had reassured himself that no robbers had entered the room would he climb the stairs wearily to bed. To bed, but not to sleep, for the horror and pain of his nightmare loss would not allow sleep to come to him again that night.

But in spite of his greed for gold, King Midas was at heart a kind man. One day, when a weary old traveller who had lost his way knocked on the golden doors of the king's palace, Midas ordered his servants to bring the man into the great dining hall.

Then Midas gave the stranger food and drink, and a couch to rest on until he was sufficiently refreshed to continue his journey.

Some days afterwards Midas was in his treasure room counting his sacks of gold coins when suddenly he sensed that there was someone in the room with him.

Who could it be? Midas looked in all the dark corners to see if a burglar could possibly have got past the guards and into the room. But the three doors of the room had triple locks on them and these were unbroken. No, he reasoned, it was impossible for any robber to have entered the room.

But someone or something was there; Midas was sure of it. Hearing a slight noise he turned in that direction and

saw a man. No, not a man, for this was no ordinary mortal. Midas immediately recognised the figure and face of the God Bacchus, come down from Mount Olympus.

Midas was astonished. Imagine seeing this great god in his treasure room. Perhaps he had heard of Midas and his collection of gold and had come to see for himself. But it was customary for a man to be silent until first addressed by the gods; so Midas just stood and waited.

Then Bacchus spoke. "Midas," he said, "you have shown great kindness to a weary stranger who came to your door. He looked to be the lowliest of men. You could never have suspected that he was my foster-father."

"Indeed, I never did," Midas assured him. "But now that I know, I am honoured to have entertained him in my house."

"You are a good man, Midas," said Bacchus, "and the gods never forget any kindnesses shown to them by man. Therefore tell me your fondest wish. Ask for it and it shall be granted!"

Midas could hardly believe his good fortune and, as you can imagine, there was only one thought in his head. "Gold, gold!" he thought to himself. "I shall ask for gold; more gold than any mortal man has ever seen."

"Oh Bacchus, my all-powerful lord," Midas pleaded, "grant that everything I touch shall turn to gold."

"Poor, frail, silly man," said Bacchus, "you have made a very foolish choice. But if that is what you want I must keep my promise and grant you your wish."

Slowly, as though dissolving in a mist, Bacchus vanished.

Midas, left alone again in his treasure room, skipped round and round the gold-filled sacks with joy.

Foolish choice, Bacchus had said. Foolish choice – nonsense! Why, with such a

gift from the gods what more could any man desire? How could anything to do with gold be foolish? Midas laughed aloud at the very idea.

Then doubt struck him. Could this wonderful thing have really happened to him? Was it all a dream – a figment of his imagination called up by his own desires? Suddenly Midas felt unsure. And how could he bear it now if this wonderful

gift was not really his to possess and cherish?

He must see if it was really true – if he really *had* the golden touch.

Midas rushed out into his garden. He spent no time at all gazing at the beauty all around him or smelling the fragrance of the exotic blooms.

He walked straight across the grass to an apple tree. He snapped a twig from the

tree and laughed with glee as he saw it turn to gold in his hand.

He plucked an apple from its bough. Oh, what a marvellous gift! In his hand he held a perfect golden apple.

He rushed into the palace and touched a big oak chair, then a rosewood table; chairs and tables, cupboards and walls. At his touch they all turned to precious, shining gold. His excitement knew no bounds.

After a while he felt that all the excitement had whetted his appetite. It was time to satisfy his hunger and quench his thirst.

He sat down at the great banqueting table, which was laden with delicious foods and wines. He raised a piece of chicken to his mouth and took a bite. His teeth grated on something as hard as stone, and one of them was almost broken in the collision. What was the matter? What careless servant was to blame for this? He would certainly reprimand him severely for risking damage to a royal tooth.

Then, taking the hard substance from his mouth, he saw that it was a piece of gold.

Struck by a terrible fear, he lifted a bunch of grapes by its stem and, putting his head back in anticipation of this refreshment, he held the grapes down so that he could pluck them off with his teeth.

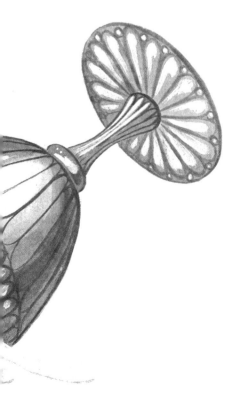

In horror he watched the lush purple ripeness change to hard glittering gold as it touched his lips.

Trembling with fear he shouted to the nearest servant, commanding him to feed his king like a baby. But this was of no avail; his whole body possessed the golden touch.

His heart was filled with terror, because he knew that he must starve to death if he could not get rid of this ability for which he had begged so earnestly.

The great fear that possessed him made his mouth dry as dust. His servant poured water into the king's wine glass to quench his thirst. But when Midas raised the goblet to his lips he dashed it to the ground with dismay, for molten gold had flown into his mouth and quickly hardened there.

Now he realised what Bacchus had meant when he had said: "You have made a very foolish choice."

What use now was all his gold if he was to perish of hunger or thirst? Too late he realised that gold was not the most precious commodity in the world; there were many other things more valuable to man, and life itself was the best gift which the gods could bestow.

"How foolish I have been!" he cried. Then he knelt down humbly and prayed to Bacchus to take back the hated gift.

For a long time he prayed without answer; then, at last, the god took pity on him.

"Go to the River Pactolus and plunge into its water," Bacchus commanded him. "Then you shall be cleansed of the golden touch. Perhaps you will also be cleansed of your greed."

Midas did not hesitate even for a second. The gift he was losing, he now realised, had never been worth having anyway. He went to the river quickly, and he came out of its waters a changed man. To his great joy he had lost the golden touch. The gold had passed from his body to the sands of the River Pactolus, and even to this day the sands still sparkle with gold.

Now that King Midas had been cured of his greed for gold he no longer spent so much time counting and gloating over his treasure. He had more time to attend to the needs of his subjects and the duties of state.

For the first time for many years he wandered into the woods and meadows, and there he met and worshipped the god Pan.

Pan was the god of all the forests and pastures and their wild life. He was an ugly but merry little man, with pointed ears and horns and legs like a goat's; he had also that animal's amazing agility. He could climb, sure-footed, up rocky

hills and down crevices, playing his pipe as he ran nimbly along. He spent much of his carefree life playing on the pipes he had made from reeds growing by the river.

Pan was not an expert musician; his talent was much less than his enthusiasm. But he enjoyed playing his pipes and his music was jolly and gay. The wood nymphs and the creatures of the forest all loved him – and so did Midas.

Pan, too, loved his own music. And the more people praised him the vainer he became, so that soon he was boasting that his skill was at least as great as that of the god Apollo, the great Sun God and the Lord of Music.

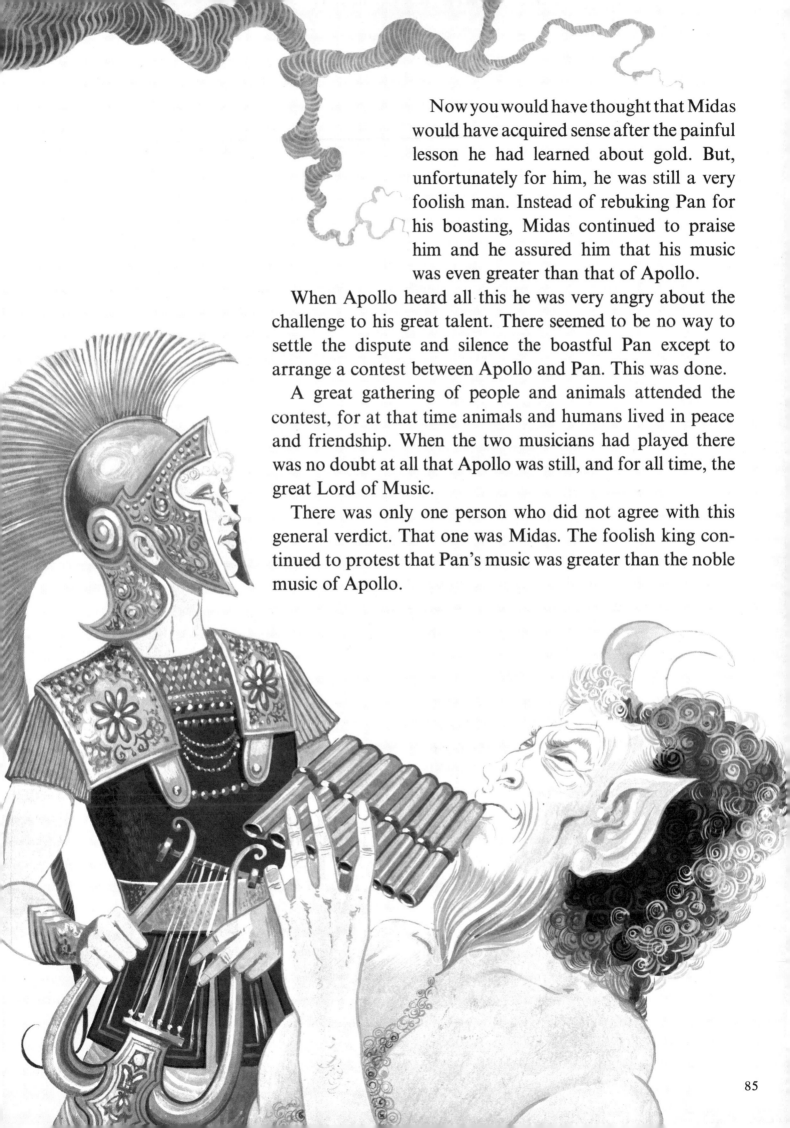

Now you would have thought that Midas would have acquired sense after the painful lesson he had learned about gold. But, unfortunately for him, he was still a very foolish man. Instead of rebuking Pan for his boasting, Midas continued to praise him and he assured him that his music was even greater than that of Apollo.

When Apollo heard all this he was very angry about the challenge to his great talent. There seemed to be no way to settle the dispute and silence the boastful Pan except to arrange a contest between Apollo and Pan. This was done.

A great gathering of people and animals attended the contest, for at that time animals and humans lived in peace and friendship. When the two musicians had played there was no doubt at all that Apollo was still, and for all time, the great Lord of Music.

There was only one person who did not agree with this general verdict. That one was Midas. The foolish king continued to protest that Pan's music was greater than the noble music of Apollo.

At first Apollo, pleased with his success and enraptured by his own music, did not pay any attention to the foolish king. But when Midas continued to protest, and ever more loudly, Apollo became very angry.

"You have made poor use of your ears," he said, looking at Midas sternly. "You are unworthy to have human ears."

Then Midas felt his ears growing long and furry: they had changed to the ears of an ass. Midas remained a human being in all other ways, but now he had an ass's ears.

This was a bitter blow to the proud king. He was terribly ashamed of his ears and he had a special purple turban which he always wore to cover them up.

But one of his servants had seen the ass's ears before they were covered. This man knew that he would be severely punished by Midas if he told anyone the shameful secret . . . but still he could not bear to keep the secret to himself.

He came to the point where he just had to speak the words. But nobody must hear him in case the rumour got around and reached the ears of the king.

So the servant went out into the middle of a field and he dug a hole in the ground and put his mouth to it. Looking round carefully to ensure that nobody was watching him, he whispered into the hole, "Midas has an ass's ears. Sh-sh-sh! Midas has an ass's ears!"

Then he carefully covered the hole with soil again and went home, happy that he was relieved of the secret and yet he had told no one.

Days and weeks passed, and eventually a crop of reeds grew up from the hole.

When the reeds grew tall they whispered in the wind, "Midas has an ass's ears. Sh-sh-sh! Midas has an ass's ears!"

Soon everyone knew the king's secret.

Midas had to pay that penalty to the gods for his second foolish act.

THE LAD WHO VISITED THE NORTH WIND

There was once a young lad named Crispin who lived with his mother in a small cottage at the end of a country lane.

One day Crispin's mother sent her son out to the storeroom in the yard to get some flour to bake some bread.

Crispin measured out the flour into a dish, but as he was crossing the yard to return indoors, the North Wind blustered along, blowing all the flour away.

Crispin went to get some more flour, and the North Wind blew this away, too.

There was now only enough flour left to make one small loaf of bread, and when the mischievous North Wind carried this flour away, Crispin got very angry.

"It is not right that we should go hungry," cried Crispin to his mother. "I shall go and see the North Wind and demand our flour back!"

So off he set. Crispin travelled many miles, for the way to the North Wind was long and often dangerous. But at last he came to the place where the North Wind lived.

"Good-day," said the lad. "I have come for my flour, for without it, we shall starve."

"Good-day to you, young sir," roared back the North Wind. "I have no flour but take, I pray you instead, that cloth which lies in yonder corner. Whenever you are hungry, say 'Cloth, spread yourself!' and every manner of good food shall be yours."

Crispin thanked the North Wind politely for his gift, and he set off home again.

On the way he stopped to rest at an inn, asking for a bed for the night.

When the other guests sat down to eat, Crispin sat down at an empty table and spread the cloth before him.

"Cloth, spread yourself!" he commanded . . . and immediately a delicious meal appeared.

The innkeeper's wife had watched the work of the magic cloth, and that night as Crispin slept she exchanged the magic cloth for one of her own tablecloths, which looked exactly like the one the North Wind had given the lad.

Next morning, suspecting nothing, Crispin bade the innkeeper and his wife a cheery farewell, and continued on his way.

When he reached home, he showed his mother the cloth and told her how it could produce food for them by magic.

But when Crispin said the magic words the cloth remained empty, and his mother chided him gently for believing in such nonsense.

This made Crispin very angry with the North Wind, and he set off to see him once again.

"The cloth was useless, and we need flour to eat!" he said to the North Wind, who was sitting on a throne looking at some weather charts.

"I have no flour," replied the North Wind. "But if you wish, you may have this goat. Say to the animal, 'Goat, make money!' and golden coins will pour from its mouth."

Crispin thanked the North Wind and started for home with his magic goat.

Once again Crispin stopped at the inn and, in order to pay for his bed for the night and some food, Crispin said to his goat, "Goat, make money!"

Immediately, golden coins poured from the animal's mouth and, watched by the amazed innkeeper and his wife, Crispin scooped them up and put them in his pocket.

That night when Crispin was fast asleep the wicked innkeeper crept outside to where the magic goat was tethered to a fence and exchanged the goat for one of his own.

Crispin left the inn, not realising that he had left his magic goat behind.

Back home again Crispin told his mother of the fine bargain he had made with the North Wind. But when he ordered the goat to make money, all the animal did was to bleat loudly and try to eat a tablecloth.

"Some fine bargain!" scoffed his mother. "I thought you had more brains than that, my son!"

This made Crispin very angry with the North Wind, and he set off to see him again, determined this time to get some flour for his mother.

"You are a hard lad to please," grumbled the North Wind when Crispin complained about his goat. "All I have left is this stick. However, it is not an ordinary stick. If you say 'Stick, lay on!' it will beat a person until you say, 'Stick, lay off!' If you wish to take it, it is yours!"

Now Crispin was quite a bright lad, and on his way to the palace of the North Wind he had realised that somehow the landlord and his wife had tricked him. It was only after he had left the inn on each occasion that his magic gifts had failed to work.

Perhaps the landlord had stolen them and replaced them with ordinary objects. If so, the magic stick might help him to get them back.

So he thanked the North Wind politely and took the stick and set off for the inn.

He kept the stick by his side all evening. The landlord, seeing this, was convinced that it was enchanted, and he determined to get it.

But as he crept into Crispin's bedchamber that night the lad was not asleep and he cried out loudly "Stick, lay on!"

And the stick began to beat the innkeeper very hard indeed!

"Give me back my magic tablecloth and the goat that makes money, and then I will tell the stick to stop!" cried Crispin.

"Wife, give the lad his tablecloth and untether the goat!" shouted the landlord.

Once the cloth and the goat were his again, Crispin called, "Stick, lay off!" The stick stopped beating the landlord and flew into Crispin's hand.

"I'll be off now," cried Crispin, as he strode out under the night sky. "With luck, I shall be home by morning, and my mother will at last see the wonderful gifts given to me by my friend, the North Wind. Now we shall not want for anything for the rest of our lives . . . and all because I visited the North Wind to ask him for my flour back!"

The Tortoise and his Friends

ALL the animals of the jungle had their own special friends, except the tortoise. He spent most of his time curled up in his hard shell, just thinking.

Eventually he began to feel rather lonely. It was time, he decided, to find himself a friend. So he looked round the jungle, carefully selecting his choice.

The lion was strong and would be able to protect him from attack. But he had his shell, into which he retreated in times of danger; besides, the lion was much too noisy a companion. The monkeys would be most unsuitable friends, too, for who had ever seen a tortoise climb a tree? And he could certainly never keep pace with a cheetah in its travels.

Finally he decided that the elephant and the hippopotamus would make ideal companions for him. These two were close friends themselves and spent much of their time together, although the elephant preferred to spend most of his time on land while the hippopotamus was happiest in the water.

Having made up his mind, the tortoise lost no time in approaching the favoured pair. "I want to join you and spend my time with you," he announced, the very next time he saw them by the river.

The elephant and his friend, the hippopotamus, were astonished, even indignant. "How can a weakling like you expect to be friends with the strongest animals in the jungle?"

"I'm stronger than either of you," claimed the tortoise, "and I'll prove it. Neither of you, however hard you pull, can pull me out of the water. Just try!"

"What cheek!" said the elephant.

"Utter nonsense!" gasped the hippopotamus.

"It's true!" The little tortoise was quite unimpressed by their anger.

"You deserve to be thrown into the water for your rudeness," said the elephant. "But to end this nonsense once and for all I'll prove my strength to you."

They found a long, strong rope in the jungle and the tortoise tied one end of it to his leg and gave the other end to the elephant. Then the tortoise dived down to the very bottom of the river.

As soon as he got there he quickly untied the rope from his leg and tied it securely round a huge boulder on the river bed. Then he sat down calmly and waited to see what would happen.

On the river bank, the elephant pulled and tugged as hard as he could; but he could not pull the tortoise up from the bottom of the river. He trumpeted and trumpeted, and got angrier and angrier, and pulled harder and

harder. In the end the rope broke and the elephant rolled head over heels into the water.

Seeing the broken rope twirling down through the water, the tortoise unfastened the end of it from the boulder and tied it again to his leg. Then he swam to the surface.

He crawled onto the bank, panting, as though exhausted. "That was a good tug-of-war," he said. "But if the rope hadn't broken when it did, I was just going to finish the contest anyway. One sharp tug and the elephant would have joined me in the water."

Many of the jungle animals had gathered to watch the contest and they all declared that the tortoise was the winner. So the elephant was forced to admit himself weaker than the tortoise.

But now it was the turn of the hippopotamus and he went to great trouble to find a stronger rope, confident that this contest would end in victory for him.

"This time I'll go into the river," said the hippopotamus, "and I shall pull you into the water after me."

"You can try," said the tortoise. "But as I

don't want another bath today I think I'll just sit in the shade at the edge of the jungle while you tire yourself out trying to pull me in."

The hippopotamus tied one end of the rope to the tortoise's back leg and the tortoise settled himself down in the long grass at the edge of the jungle.

Then the hippopotamus dived to the bottom of the river and started to pull as hard as he could.

But, as soon as the hippopotamus was in the water, the tortoise untied the rope from his leg and fastened it to the sturdy palm tree under which he was sitting.

The hippopotamus tugged and tugged until every muscle in his powerful body ached. At last, when he was so tired he could hardly swim, he came out of the river and scrambled, gasping, up the bank.

Immediately, the tortoise, who had been watching every ripple of the water, took the rope end from the palm tree and quickly fastened it around his leg again.

"You see," he said to the hippopotamus, as he made a great show of unfastening the rope in front of the big animal, "even after all that pulling my leg is still strong and not at all sore."

The hippopotamus was gracious in defeat. "Indeed, you have proved that you are stronger than either of us. You may live with us and be our friend for ever."

"I shall live with the elephant," said the tortoise. "But my son can live with you. For I prefer the dry land, while he likes the water."

To this very day, there are water-tortoises as well as land-tortoises. And now *you* know how it all began.

The Musicians of Bremen

A certain ass had served his master for many long years, carrying and pulling for him and demanding very little attention in return. But now he was growing old and his strength was failing rapidly so that he was unable to do most of the work for which he was fitted.

One day, as he was grazing in a field, he heard his master say: "The old ass is no good for work now, but perhaps I could get enough money for his skin to buy a new ass for myself."

The ass didn't favour this idea at all. So, with strength he didn't know he possessed, he kicked up his heels, jumped over the hedge and ran down the road so fast that the farmyard cat stopped washing herself and made for cover. She thought the ass was being pursued by a demon, for indeed she hadn't seen him run so fast for years.

Down the road he trotted, his legs crossing each other in a half-drunken stagger in his anxiety to escape from his cruel master.

He would go to Bremen, he decided, and try his luck there as a musician. "There they will appreciate my fine musical voice," he thought to himself. And he brayed loud and clear for all to hear.

Just as he was slowing down to a weary jog he saw a dog lying by the roadside, yawning and panting.

"What ails you, my friend?" asked the ass.

"Oh, mine is a sad tale," replied the dog. "Once I used to hunt daily with my master.

But now every day I am getting older and weaker. My master wanted to have me destroyed, so I have run away. But, alas, I do not know of any way to earn my bread."

"I sympathize with you," said the ass, "but you must not despair. Join me, for I am going to Bremen to try my luck as a musician."

"I would like to join you," said the dog, "and I might be of some help to you for I have a fine musical voice." And he barked loudly.

They had scarcely gone a few yards down the road when they came to a black cat with a face as cheerless as three rainy days.

"What's the matter with you?" asked the ass.

"I am growing old," said the black cat, "and my teeth are worn to stumps. Once I was a fine mouser but now I would rather lie by the fire than chase mice. So my mistress thinks me useless and would have me drowned. That is why I have run away."

"Join your companions in misfortune," said the ass. "I have heard that you waken the neighbourhood with your voice at night, and we are going to Bremen to be town musicians."

"That would suit me very well," said the cat, preening herself. "I have a very musical voice." And she mewed shrilly but quite pleasantly.

The three hopeful musicians journeyed on together, and presently they came to a farmyard. A cock with a bright red comb was perched on the barn door, crowing with all his might.

"What are you crowing so loudly about?" asked the ass, who is really quite an intelligent and curious animal, despite what people say.

"I am crowing as hard as I can while there is still breath in me." As the cock told them his sad tale he didn't sound nearly as gay as his crowing had done.

"This morning," he said, "I arose early, as I always do. It was a beautiful morning and I awoke the farmer's wife by crowing out that it was fine weather for haymaking. But she did not thank me for my trouble and later I heard that she is going to make me into soup for tomorrow's dinner."

"We cannot leave you to such a terrible fate," said the ass. "Come away and join us. We are going to Bremen to try our luck as musicians. We all know that you have a splendid voice and if we make music together it should sound very well."

So the four travellers started on the road to Bremen again: the long-eared ass, the brown dog, the sleek black cat and the cock with his bright red comb.

Soon they realised that they could not reach Bremen that day so when evening came they decided to spend the night in a forest. The ass and the dog lay down wearily under a tall tree; the cat climbed up into the branches to sleep, while the cock flew right to the top of the tree, where he felt safest.

Before settling down to sleep he looked all around him. He noticed a pinprick of light not far away and, calling his companions, he told them that there was a house nearby.

"Well, then," said the ass, "let us see if we can find shelter there, for there is not enough grass round here to provide a decent supper."

The brown dog agreed. "A couple of juicy bones would be most acceptable," he said.

Following the cock's instructions they arrived at the house. The ass went up to the window and peered inside.

"What do you see, Long Ears?" asked the cock.

"I see a table covered with good food and drink," replied the ass. "And sitting round the table I see a band of robbers."

"If only we could get into the house," sighed his companions.

Then the four animals took counsel together and made a bold plan to drive away the robbers. The ass placed his forefeet upon the window-ledge; the dog climbed up on his back; the cat leapt up on the dog's shoulders and, finally, the cock flew up and perched on the cat's head.

Then, at a signal from the ass, they began to perform their music: the ass brayed, the dog barked, the cat mewed and the cock crew. It may not have been great music but it was a terrific noise!

Then they all burst through the window, shattering the glass into a myriad of sparkling pieces.

Terrified at the noise and the unearthly

vision at the window, the robbers scrambled from the table, trembling with fear, and fled into the wood.

The four travelling musicians sat down and ate and drank all that was left on the table, as though they had been fasting for weeks.

Later they put out the lamp, and each found himself a sleeping place, according to his nature and custom. The ass lay down on a heap of straw; the dog stretched out behind the door; the cat curled up beside the kitchen fire, and the cock flew up into the rafters. Soon they were all asleep.

Meanwhile, out in the forest, the robbers were watching the house. By the time the light went out they had got over their first fright.

"We ran away like scared children," said the robber chief, "and perhaps it was just some trick being played on us. Anyway it seems quiet enough now." And he sent one of his band back to the house to find out what had happened.

When the messenger arrived at the house all was still. Opening the door quietly he went into the kitchen. Intending to light the lamp he took out a match from his pocket. He saw the fiery, glistening eyes of the cat as she crouched beside the hearth and, mistaking them for live coals, he held the match out to them.

At once the cat sprang at him, spitting and scratching. The terrified robber ran to the door, where the dog jumped up and bit his leg. As he limped through the yard the ass jumped up from his bed of straw

and kicked him. Then the cock, wakened by all the noise, cried out from the rafters: *"Cock-a-doodle-do!"*

The robber hobbled and ran, ran and hobbled, as fast as he could, back to his companions.

He was shaking with fright as he recounted his experiences. "There is a horrible old witch in the kitchen who spat at me and scratched me with her long fingernails. Behind the door stands a man with a knife, who chopped at my leg. In the yard lies a black monster, who jumped at me and beat me with a great wooden club. And from the rafters the devil himself cried, 'Bring the knave up, do!'. So I ran away as fast as I could."

When they heard this frightening tale, the robbers left the place and never returned. But the long-eared ass, the brown dog, the sleek black cat and the cock with the bright red comb found the house suited them so well that they gave up the idea of becoming musicians in Bremen and decided to stay in the robbers' house. And, as far as I know, they are still living there.

The Thief of Bagdad

Once upon a time, a young orphan boy named Hassan lived in the ancient city of Bagdad. He had no parents and kept himself alive by stealing from the rich merchants who travelled to the city each day to sell their wares. Every night he would sleep under the walls of the mosque that overshadowed the city.

Day after day, Hassan lived in this way, and sometimes the Caliph's men, called by the merchants, would see him and try to catch him. They would chase him through the city crying, "Stop thief!" but, of course, Hassan ran the faster to escape from them. They never caught him.

When he felt safe, he would empty his pockets of all he had stolen. There would be loaves, fruit and often a bottle of wine. One day, leaning against a tree, Hassan ate some bread and fruit, then took the cork from an oldish-looking bottle. There was a faint pop and a hissing noise. As he bent forward to sniff the contents, to his amazement, vapour from the bottle curled out and rose up, bigger and bigger, higher and higher into the sky!

Writhing this way and that, the vapour suddenly turned into an enormous man towering above him. Poor Hassan shook with fear as he looked up at the huge figure, for he knew not whether the giant was good or evil.

Smiling, the giant looked down at the trembling boy and said, "Don't be afraid for I am your slave. Whatever you command, I will obey." He held out his hand.

Hassan knew then, that it was no dream.

When Hassan had got over his surprise and fright he said, "Take me to the Caliph's Palace, so that I may see the beautiful Princess."

"Climb on my back, little master, and hold on tight," said the slave and soon they were flying over the rooftops of the city. How exciting it was!

Hassan held on tightly for he was still just a little bit scared. The city looked so tiny far below him and the slave seemed to fly very fast. He had to pinch himself to make sure that he was not imagining it all. Only a few minutes ago he had been a poor orphan boy being chased out of the city and now here he was flying!

The slave began to slow down and circle gently round the Caliph's Palace, the towers shining in the evening light. They glided down to a big, open window.

"There," whispered the slave and lowered Hassan to the floor. Looking round in wonder he found himself in a fine bedroom with rich hangings, a tiger-skin rug on the floor, a golden bed and, wonder of wonders, there was the Princess. She lay fast asleep in her beautiful bed, her soft, black hair hanging in a cloud round her pillow.

At once Hassan fell in love with her; straight away, he knew he loved her dearly. Looking down at his poor clothes, he knew he must hide or he might wake and frighten her. But as he turned, he bumped into a small table, and the slight sound woke the sleeping girl.

"Don't be afraid, I just wanted to see you," he said, "my name is Hassan. I will not hurt you."

"Go quickly, or the guards will find you," she said.

"Farewell, lovely Princess, I shall not forget you." And Hassan climbed out of the window into the city darkness.

The Princess turned over in bed and thought of Hassan. He had not frightened her and she wondered about him. She was engaged to marry Prince Genghis of the Red Plume, but she did not love him. She was frightened of him for he was cruel and scheming. He was already plotting the downfall of her father once he married the Princess, for he wanted his rich kingdom very badly.

The Caliph knew his child was unhappy and told Prince Genghis that she must decide the wedding date, but the Prince was very angry and demanded they marry at the next full moon. He told the Princess that unless she agreed he would send his army, which was very strong, to fight her father's small force, and take over her peace-loving country.

The Princess was very unhappy for she knew she loved Hassan. In despair, she told her father she could not marry Prince Genghis, whatever happened.

"Father, I love Hassan," she wept, "I hate Prince Genghis. He is cruel and wicked. I cannot marry him."

"Who is Hassan?" asked the Caliph, "is he a prince?"

"He is a poor little thief from Bagdad," she replied.

"A thief!" cried the Caliph.

"I met him the other day, but I will marry him, for, in spite of everything, I know he is good and honest."

Prince Genghis, who had been listening outside the door, heard the Princess's words and burst in.

"You want to marry a thief!" he cried. "I'll find him and hang him, the rogue! How dare you prefer a guttersnipe to a Prince of my greatness," he roared.

"No, stop, please," begged the Princess, "don't hurt him."

"Hurt him!" sneered Prince Genghis, "I'll kill him."

He laughed, an evil, menacing sound as he turned to go from the room.

Suddenly, a strong wind blew through the Palace, fluttering the curtains, banging the windows, ruffling the rich wall hangings.

Out of nowhere, Hassan appeared wearing fine silks and satins and smiling at the Princess who ran to greet him. He looked very handsome in his rich clothes.

Everyone else gasped in amazement for behind Hassan stood the tallest giant they had ever seen. It was his slave of the bottle.

"I am Hassan," the boy said," I have come to ask for the hand of the Princess in marriage." And he walked up to the Caliph's throne.

"This man is a thief," cried Prince Genghis, "seize him," he told the guards.

As the guards moved to obey, the Prince snatched up a sword himself and rushed to attack Hassan.

Swiftly, the giant lifted up the struggling Prince, opened a window, and, holding him high in the air, flung him up into the sky. He was never seen again.

The Caliph realised how wicked Prince Genghis had been and threw his arms round his beloved daughter, telling her she and Hassan could be married — even if he was a thief, though he doubted so great a man could be one.

Hassan fell on his knees and thanked the Caliph, then he held the Princess in his arms.

The giant smiled. Hassan looked at him and thanked him for all he had done. "Is there anything I can do for you in return?" he asked. "Can I give you anything?"

"My freedom," the giant replied.

"You have it," said Hassan, "go and do good all over the world, my friend. I shall never forget you." With a wave of his hand, the giant disappeared in a cloud.

"He's gone," said Hassan sadly as he gazed out of the window at the rising cloud.

"Never mind, he brought us together," reminded the Princess, and that made them both smile again.

The Caliph put the wedding preparations in hand straight away and there was great rejoicing throughout the land.

Hassan and his Princess lived happily ever after, but he often thought of his faithful slave and wondered who he was helping. Whenever he opened a bottle, he always took special care, just in case he might find another slave inside.

Puss in Boots

Many years ago, an old miller died leaving his son, Tom, a black cat — that was all! This was no ordinary cat, though. He was a very special cat indeed. Not only was he very clever but he was able to talk as well!

"Master," he said, "don't be unhappy. Trust me, and I will make you rich."

"But, Puss, what can you do?" said Tom, feeling sad.

"You just leave everything to me," said Puss.

"Oh well, I've nothing to lose," laughed Tom.

"Just buy me some boots — red I think — a cape and a hat with a feather," said Puss. He looked very smart.

With a cheery wave, Puss slung a sack over his shoulder and set off. On his way, he stopped by the river and waited for a fat fish to swim by. Quick as a flash, he scooped it out of the water and put it into his sack. Then he walked to the King's Palace.
"Take me to the King," he commanded the footman.

Puss swept off his plumed hat with a flourish and bowed low before the King.
"My Master, the Marquis of Carabas, presents his compliments to Your Majesty and hopes you will accept this gift."

The King was delighted. He wondered who the Marquis of Carabas could be, for he had never heard of him. Little did he think he was Tom, a poor miller's son!

Every day, Puss brought more fish or game to the King — rabbits, pheasants, plump partridges, — all from his Master. So the King wanted to meet the Marquis and Puss had to think of a plan. He must find some finery for Tom, somehow.

Puss learned that every day the King and his lovely daughter drove past the river in the Royal Coach. He told Tom to bathe in the river next afternoon, and, trusting his clever cat, he did so.

At once, Puss seized Tom's clothes and hid them. As the royal coach approached, Puss rushed up and down the path looking worried.

"My poor Master, he is drowning! Help!" he cried.

The Royal Coach stopped and the King recognised Puss. When he heard the Marquis was in danger, he ordered his men to rescue Tom from the river. Puss pretended to search for his clothes and said that they had been stolen. The King ordered one of his men to lend Tom a cloak and he was able to climb out on to the bank.

"You shall have a royal suit of clothes," cried the King and sent his men back to the Palace to fetch one for Tom.

"Thank you very much," said Tom. "You are so kind."

When the suit arrived, it fitted Tom perfectly and he looked very smart. Puss felt very proud as he introduced the Marquis to the King.

"I am so glad to meet you and have a chance to thank you for those wonderful presents of game you have been sending me," said the King shaking Tom's hand.

Tom looked amazed. What on earth was the King talking about? Marquis? Presents! He must be mad. Puss gave him a fierce nudge so his master knew it was part of the plan to make him rich, so he smiled at the King.

"May I present my daughter, the Princess?" said the King. She was such a beautiful girl that Tom immediately fell in love with her.

"Come back to the Palace," the King invited Tom.

One of the courtiers had told Puss that all the lands nearby belonged to a terrible ogre who was a magician living in a huge castle. So Puss thought of another plan.

Running on ahead, he told all the reapers and workers in the fields to say that the lands belonged to the Marquis of Carabas and that he would reward them. The men willingly agreed, as did those in the vineyard, so the King was most impressed as he rode by to learn all the lands were Tom's.

Meanwhile, Puss had gone on to the ogre's castle. Bravely he marched into the great hall where the ogre was sitting.

The ogre laughed when he saw Puss in all his finery and, though this was rude, the clever cat decided to try flattery.

"I hear you are a great magician, sir," he said humbly.

"I am the greatest!" boasted the Ogre.

"The greatest?" echoed Puss in wonder.

"I can do anything, anything at all I want," said the Ogre.

"I wonder if anyone can be so clever," said Puss daringly.

"Do you dare to doubt me? I can do *anything!*" roared the Ogre jumping up in a fury. Puss was just a bit scared.

"Can you change into an animal, for instance?" he asked.

"An animal, that's easy," said the Ogre.

He stood up, all seven feet of him, and muttered some strange words. There was a silence as Puss watched.

What would happen next?

He soon found out, for with a roar, the Ogre turned into an enormous lion. He looked so fierce with his teeth bared and his paws raised that Puss, in his surprise, fell off his chair! When he had suggested an animal he had no idea the Ogre would turn into a lion! What could he do now?

The lion jumped straight at Puss roaring in his rage, but the cat quickly hid under the table making himself as small as possible. The great beast roared and growled trying to hit Puss with his great paws.

Puss thought hard. Maybe he could bring the Ogre back.

"Can you change back?" he asked. In a flash the Ogre was there!

"That was clever," said Puss admiringly.

"I told you I could do anything," said the Ogre, smiling and pleased with himself.

"But, surely, it is easy for someone as big as yourself to turn into a large animal, you have to be *really* clever to turn into a small animal?" said Puss.

"Nonsense! I can do anything I wish," boasted the Ogre.

"Could you, for instance, turn into something very small, something like a mouse?" asked Puss, cunningly.

"Watch me!" cried the Ogre.

Once more he stood up and uttered the magic words. Hey presto! instead of the Ogre a tiny mouse scampered across the floor.

This was just what Puss had hoped for. Swiftly he pounced on the mouse and gobbled him up — and that was the end of the Ogre! Now he had to make the castle ready to receive his master and, later, the King and Princess.

Puss called all the servants of the castle into the great hall and told them how he had killed the wicked Ogre. They were overjoyed at the news, for the Ogre had been a cruel master and their life had been hard.

"Our Master, the Marquis of Carabas, is staying with the King and Princess, but they are coming here as guests. You must make ready and prepare a great banquet." Everyone set to work with a will and a huge feast was prepared. Meanwhile, Puss had got word to Tom who marvelled at what he saw. When all was ready, Puss told his master to invite the King and Princess to visit his castle.

When the King and the Princess arrived they were delighted with everything. Puss, who was in charge of the staff, had found a huge store of gold and silver in the vaults of the castle, so that his master was now a rich man.

The Princess and the Marquis soon fell in love and when the King gave his blessing to their marriage they were overjoyed.

At the wedding, the Princess and Marquis made a handsome pair and Puss, dressed in a new velvet suit, proudly carried the train.

The Marquis and Princess were very happy, and Puss was a great hero. He and his master went all over the kingdom, deposing the wicked ogres and barons, and soon there was peace and happiness everywhere. How the people cheered the noble Marquis and his faithful Puss!

Tom never forgot he was just a miller's son and always helped the poor and needy whenever he could; everyone grew to love him as a wise and kind man. But he knew he owed it all to Puss without whose help he would still have been at the old mill.

The Marquis and Princess had a large family and lived happily ever after. As for Puss, he found himself a Pussy Princess with long whiskers and soft, soft fur, so he was very happy, too. He smiles now when he remembers the old days at the mill, and what might have been!

MASTER of all MASTERS

One day a young girl went to the fair. She was poor and needed work, so she was looking for someone who would hire her as a servant.

On the very same day an old man went to the fair; he was looking for someone to do his housework.

As luck would have it – and luck is wonderfully useful for a storyteller – the young girl and the old man met at the fair. After some discussion, which might even be termed argument, they struck a bargain as to the girl's wages. So she went home with him that very day.

Now the minute they entered the house the old man turned to the girl. "Sit down, lass," he said, "and listen to me very carefully. In this house I have my own names for things, and if you do not call my things by these names I will forbid you to talk. Now, then, what will you call *me*?"

The poor girl was quite bewildered; she had never heard such strange talk before. "I shall call you master, or mister, or whatever you like, sir," she said.

"No, never," said he. "You must call me Master of all Masters. And what will you call this?" He pointed a long bony finger at the bed.

"I suppose I would call it bed or bunk – or whatever you like, sir," she answered him.

"That's my Barnacle, lass. Remember, Barnacle. How would you name these?" He pointed to his baggy trousers.

"Maybe pantaloons or baggytoons," suggested the girl, hopefully.

"Squibs and Crackers, lass. Never anything else but Squibs and Crackers."

Just then the cat came into the room. "What will you call her?" asked the old man.

"*I* would call her cat or kitty, but I'm willing to abide by whatever name you give her, sir."

"Whitefaced Siminy, that's her name," he said, and then he pointed to the fire. "And what do you think you'll be calling that?"

"Fire or flame, or maybe fuel-eater. Anyway, whatever name you like, sir."

"Hot Cockalorum it is, my lass. Remember now, Hot Cockalorum. And what do you think this is?" said he, pointing to a bucket of water that stood in the corner.

"Oh, whatever you like, sir," said the girl, by now tired of this game. "Perhaps water or drink."

"No, no, that is Pondalorum. And what do you call all this?" he asked, waving his hand to include the whole house.

"Please, sir, I'll call it whatever you wish. But *I* would have called it home or house."

"High Topper Mountain, you must call it, High Topper Mountain. And see that you do, or else hold your tongue."

The poor girl made and served the supper without saying one word, for she was afraid of saying the wrong thing.

The old man ate up every bite, and then went to bcd and fell sound asleep.

But during the night the girl shook him wide awake, crying, "Master of all Masters, get out of your Barnacle quickly and put on your Squibs and Crackers. White-faced Siminy has got a spark on her tail, and unless you get some more Pondalorum, High Topper Mountain will be all Hot Cockalorum."

HANS in LUCK

There was once a youth named Hans who hired himself out to his master for seven years. During this time Hans worked hard and honestly. But when the seven years had ended, Hans went to his master and said, "Master, my term of hiring is finished. Now I would like to return to my own village to see my mother once again."

"And so you shall, Hans," replied his master. "You have served me well for seven years, and now you shall have your reward."

And his master gave Hans a real piece of gold, as big as the youth's head.

Hans thanked his master for the gold. Then he wrapped it in a large kerchief and, swinging his bundle over his shoulder, Hans set off home.

But as he walked along, the lump of gold seemed to grow heavier and heavier with each step, until poor Hans began to wilt in the hot sun.

Suddenly up rode a man on a horse and cantered along beside Hans.

"I wish I could ride on a horse instead of walking along with this lump of gold," said Hans to the horseman.

The man's eyes gleamed at the mention of gold and he said, "If you like, my fine fellow, I will give you my horse for your piece of gold."

"Gladly, sir, if you are sure the bargain will suit you," replied Hans with a merry laugh.

So Hans handed over his gold and the man helped Hans onto the horse.

"Gee up!" cried the man, slapping the horse on its flank, and off it went.

Hans was delighted to travel on horseback without the heavy weight of the gold dragging him down. For a time all went well, until suddenly the loud buzzing of a bee frightened the horse and it bolted.

Hans would have taken a nasty tumble if a peasant, leading a cow, had not caught the horse's reins and forced it to stop.

Hans jumped down from the horse and he glared angrily at the animal.

"You are a prankish nag!" he cried crossly. "I wish I had a docile cow to give me milk and butter instead. A cow would not run away with me!

"Then take my cow and I will take your horse!" cried the peasant.

And so the bargain was struck.

As Hans drove his cow along the road in front of him, he came to an inn where he stopped for something to eat. The meal made him thirsty, so Hans decided to milk his cow.

He borrowed a pail from the innkeeper, and tried to milk the animal . . . but try as he might, Hans could not get even one drop of milk.

The cow got impatient with Hans and gave him a kick in the stomach, sending poor Hans tumbling to the ground.

A boy who was driving a pig on the road nearby burst out laughing.

"Old Molly hates to part with her milk!" he chuckled. "You'd be better off with a pig like mine."

"Will you give me your pig for this cow?" asked Hans, eagerly.

"Well, I reckon I could learn to milk old Molly," grinned the boy. "It's a bargain!"

So off Hans went towards the village where he lived, driving the pig before him as he walked along.

Presently he met a goosegirl with a plump white goose under her arm.

"Isn't this a fine goose?" she cried to Hans. "It is the best in the flock. Don't you wish it was yours?"

"Indeed I do!" cried Hans, eyeing the goose enviously.

"Well, we do have lots of geese, but not one pig," said the girl. "Here, take the goose and I'll take your pig!"

"Willingly," cried Hans, and once again the bargain was made.

And so Hans travelled on with his goose tucked firmly beneath his arm. As he came to the outskirts of his village Hans met a knife-grinder, seated beneath a hedge, whirling his wheel and singing:

"Silver scissors and cooks' knives I grind,
A sharper fellow is hard to find."

"You seem content with your life, Knife-grinder," said Hans.

"Indeed I am," agreed the grinder. "But what a fine goose you have there. Where did you buy it?"

"I exchanged it for my pig," explained Hans, and he went on to tell the knife-grinder about the bargains he had made with the cow, the horse and the lump of gold.

As he listened, the grinder realised that Hans was rather a simpleton, who might easily be persuaded to part with his fine goose.

"If you give me your goose, I will give you a stone to start you off as a knife-grinder," he said to Hans. "Soon you will have lots of money in your pocket. What do you say, lad?"

"How can you ask me?" cried Hans. "A pocketful of money for my goose, and a job for life! Here, take the goose!"

The knife-grinder seized the goose, and in exchange he gave Hans a large stone which was lying in the hedge.

"There is your stone, take great care of it!" cried the man as he hurried off with the goose and his grinding wheel in the opposite direction.

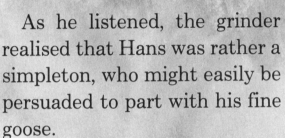

Happy with his bargain, Hans put the heavy stone in his pocket and set off again. But as he passed over the packhorse bridge which spanned the river, the stone felt very heavy in his pocket.

Some ducks were swimming on the river, and as Hans leaned over the bridge to take a closer look at them the stone slipped out of his pocket and fell into the river with a big splash.

Hans watched the stone sink to the bottom . . . and then he laughed.

"That stone was weighing me down. How lucky I am that it fell in the river!" he cried.

And with a light heart he ran happily up the path of his mother's cottage.

The Sleeping Beauty

Many years ago, there lived a King and Queen who had no children. So there was great rejoicing in the whole land when their daughter, with her fair, golden hair, blue eyes and soft, pinky skin, was born.

The King gave a huge Christening party, inviting all the nobles and not forgetting the six good fairies who lived in the kingdom. Everyone came from far and wide.

It was a wonderful party. All the guests brought special gifts for the little Princess and marvelled at her loveliness as she lay in her cradle.

The six good fairies smiled at the sleeping child. The King had six golden plates specially made for them so they felt very important. The fairy godmothers each gave the baby their blessings — a special wish for her. One promised beauty, another wisdom, the third health, the fourth happiness and the fifth good manners. The sixth fairy waited her turn.

Then there was a terrible noise. Into the room stormed a very powerful wizard who was so angry he had not been invited to the party. In the bustle he had been forgotten! "You shall pay for this!" he shouted, "I will not be insulted. I shall curse the child!"

Lifting a thin, bony finger he pointed it at the child. Everyone

held their breath. "One day, something sharp will prick the Princess's finger and when that happens, you will all go to sleep for ever." In a puff of smoke he disappeared.

The King at once ordered that no pins, needles or spinning wheels be allowed in the kingdom, and for years all was well. The Princess grew into a beautiful girl.

On her sixteenth birthday, she was wandering through the Palace when she came upon a room in which an old lady sat spinning. The old lady had found the spinning wheel in an attic and had forgotten the King's order. The Princess had never seen a spinning wheel before.

"Oh, please may I try?" she begged, "do let me see if I can do it, it looks so easy."

The old lady handed her the spindle and at once she pricked her finger. Terrified she ran to the King and Queen, but already the spell was working. Everyone was yawning.

Soon the whole Palace was asleep. The cook went to sleep stirring the soup, the King and Queen slept as they sat on their thrones, their courtiers lying snoring at their feet. The maids dropped the dusters they held and dropped on to the floor. Even the dogs and cats stopped fighting each other and lay down, their eyes shut. The soldiers, who were supposed to guard the Palace, stood at attention, fast asleep! Nothing in the whole place stirred for everyone was in a deep, deep sleep. Not a sound could be heard anywhere.

The terrible curse of the wicked wizard had come true — if only someone had invited him to the party!

Then, along came the sixth fairy who had not yet given the Princess her blessing. She touched everything with her magic wand. "Sleep not for ever," she said," you shall be awakened, a hundred years from now, when a handsome Prince kisses the Princess." And she flew off.

So the long, hundred years passed by. The dust settled and the cobwebs grew throughout the sleeping palace. Untroubled, the Princess and the whole Court slumbered on in the silence.

One day, a handsome young Prince rode into the kingdom with his followers. As they mounted a rise, they saw the old Palace silently standing on its hilltop. As they drew nearer, they passed reapers in the fields asleep with their scythes, and goats, sheep and cows standing like statues.

"I don't like it," said one of the men, "they are all bewitched. Let's ride away at once."

"It's too strange to be true," said another, "we'd better ride back the way we came."

But the Prince was filled with curiosity and, putting spurs to his horse rode up to the castle, calling out for a groom to take his animal. "I'm going inside," he said and rushed up the stairs, passed the sleeping guards.

Once inside, he found it silent and echoing with sentries, maids, courtiers, even dogs, apparently asleep. He tried to wake them, shaking them and calling but no one stirred.

His men at his heels, they went from room to room but everything was silent and still. "There must be magic afoot," murmured the Prince, drawing his sword, but he went on searching for an answer.

At last, he came to the bedroom where the sleeping Princess lay, her fair hair streaming over the pillow.

"Wake, wake up," he called, drawing the curtains to let in the sunlight, and touched her face with his hand. He called again, louder this time.

"Wake up, wake up," but she did not stir.

"Let's all clap our hands and shout, and perhaps the noise will awaken her," suggested one of his friends.

"Wa----ke up, wa----ke up," they all chorused, again and again. It seemed nothing could wake her.

Turning away in despair, for she was so beautiful, the Prince felt two tears slide slowly down his cheeks.

He knew he must kiss her goodbye before he left.

He bent down and kissed her gently, then stood for a moment, gazing at her. How pale she looked and how cold her lips!

The Prince stared at her sadly, then, to his great joy, her eyelids began to flutter and her blue eyes opened.

"Where am I?" she whispered, sitting up and looking at him.

"Don't be afraid!" he cried, "you are quite safe at home."

"But everything is strange!" she said, "What has happened?"

"I have broken the spell," the Prince told her. "My lovely Princess is awake once more." And his friends came to look at her, sharing his delight at her beauty.

"It is all like a dream," she said.

"Perhaps it has been a dream, for everyone is asleep," he said.

Then the Princess remembered.

"It must be the Wizard's spell," she exclaimed, "years ago he put a curse on my family and said we would sleep for ever." She was just about to jump out of bed to see if her parents still slept and if the Prince had really broken the spell, when the King and

Queen and courtiers walked into the room, laughing and talk-ing.

With a glad cry, the Princess rushed to her mother and threw her arms round her neck."Mother," she cried, and then kissed her father who stood smiling at everyone.

"The spell is broken!" cried the King, and indeed it was, for the whole Palace was filled with the sounds of laughter, the dogs barked once more and the fields were echoing to the mooing of cows.

"This is the Prince who has rescued us," said the Princess, taking him by the hand and presenting him to her parents.

"My dear Prince," cried the King, "how can I reward you, for you have saved us all?"

"I should like to marry your daughter," the Prince replied and kissed the Princess again. She smiled her happiness, for he was the most handsome Prince she had ever seen.

Plans for the grandest wedding in the kingdom were made and all was bustle in the Palace. The royal bakers made a special cake, and such a feast was prepared the like of which had never been seen before. Invitations were sent far and wide, to the fairies and, because the King was not going to make another mistake, a special messenger carried one to the wizard.

The Prince and Princess were married amid great rejoicing and the bells pealed their welcome. The celebrations were at their height when a sudden silence fell on the room. In walked the wizard, dressed in his finest clothes!

"So!" he said, "you have learned your lesson! If you had remembered your manners all those years ago, I should not have been so cross, and you would not have had a hundred years' sleep!" He laughed. "I shall make another spell."

Everyone gasped. What would he do now?

"Remember the fairies' blessings at the Christening?" he said, "well my spell will make them all come true!

"You will both have health, wealth and happiness all your days."

So everyone was very happy and the King forgave the Wizard for being so horrid by giving him a special present.

The end of a Friendship

MANY years ago, the elephant and the tiger were the best of friends. But that was before they learned that betting, between friends, is a dangerous pastime.

It all began one morning as they walked together through the dense jungle. They were discussing all sorts of grave issues, for both the tiger and the elephant sat on the high council which, under the supreme authority of the lion, ruled the jungle. But today the friends'

serious discussions were disturbed by a little monkey who was leaping through the branches above them, chattering all the while.

"Be quiet!" roared the tiger.

"Silence!" trumpeted the elephant.

But the little monkey took not the slightest notice.

The elephant lost patience. "We must teach this monkey manners," he said. "Let us frighten him so much that he falls down from the tree."

It was the tiger who suggested that they make a bet on it. "If I cannot do it, you may eat me up. And if you cannot do it, then I will eat you up."

"Agreed," said the elephant.

"Then you begin," said the tiger.

So the elephant began to behave as if he had lost his wits, circling around the tree in which the monkey was perched and trumpeting so loudly that the earth shook.

The monkey, terrified by the din, jumped from branch to branch. Yet he did not drop to the ground.

The elephant continued until his throat was hoarse.

"Now it's your turn," he gasped to the tiger. "But don't forget, he must actually drop to the ground."

The tiger began to growl, snarl, grunt and roar. Then he made as if to spring into the tree.

The monkey became so crazed with fear that he lost his grip on the branch and dropped to the ground, directly in front of the tiger.

"You have won," groaned the elephant. "But let me have a week in which to say good-bye to my family and settle my affairs."

The tiger agreed and the elephant went home. For seven days he did not eat, nor drink, nor sleep. All he did was trumpet and trumpet and trumpet. All the animals came to see what was the matter; but when they heard they shook their heads sadly and went away.

News travels fast in the jungle – almost as fast as the beat of a drum. Yet it was the seventh day before the musk deer heard about the sad affair.

He hurried to the elephant's home, where his friend was even now taking a tearful leave of his family.

"I would be very sorry to lose you, friend elephant," said the musk deer. "We must certainly think of some way to save you."

"If you only can," pleaded the elephant, "I shall be your servant for life and so shall all my relatives."

The clever little musk deer set to work quickly. Getting a big bottle of palm syrup he poured it over the elephant's back, letting the red syrup run down his sides and legs.

"Now I will ride on your back," said the musk deer. "And, as I am licking the syrup off your back, you must trumpet as loudly as you can and wriggle from side to side as though you were in terrible pain."

So they set off through the jungle, the elephant making as loud and as miserable a noise as if the musk deer was indeed eating him alive.

When they arrived at the meeting place the tiger was already there.

"A tiger!" exclaimed the musk deer, smacking its lips. "And a fat one too. That might satisfy my hunger better than this leathery old elephant."

Hearing these words and listening to the screams of the elephant, the tiger quickly fled.

Crashing through the underbrush he met the great black ape.

"Who's chasing you?" asked the ape. He was rather annoyed because, being slow-moving, he had been nearly knocked down by the tiger's onslaught.

"Oh, please do not delay me," gasped the tiger. "The most terrible creature is eating my dear friend the elephant, who should have been my supper tonight. And this creature threatened to eat me too. I must get home quickly!"

"Indeed," muttered the ape, half to himself. "This sounds just like my old school friend, the musk deer. He was always playing tricks – quite a clever little fellow for his size!"

The ape persuaded the tiger to go back with him into the jungle. "You need not be afraid, I will protect you," he promised the tiger.

Soon they met the musk deer, riding on the elephant's back and licking up the syrup.

But the musk deer was a quick thinker. "Hello, Uncle Ape," he shouted in greeting. "You've let me down, I see. You promised to bring me three tigers and all you've brought me is one, and an old one at that. I'll make a

start with that, it will have to do for a first course."

Hearing this, the tiger turned tail and fled for his life. "Miserable rogue!" he roared back at the ape. "You tried to trick me so that your friend could have me for his supper. If ever you cross my path again, I shall eat you myself."

The tiger ran into the jungle, and he probably hasn't stopped running yet. But from that day on the tiger and the ape have been deadly enemies.